The Miniature World of
MARVIN
& JAMES

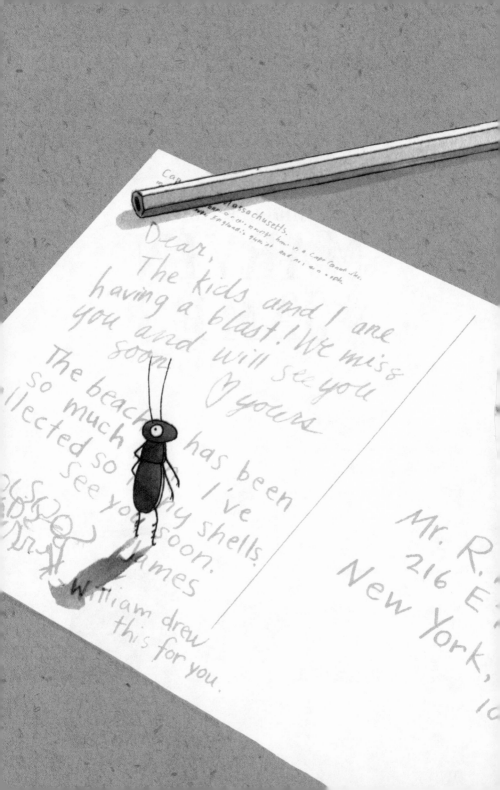

SQUARE
FISH

An Imprint of Macmillan
175 Fifth Avenue
New York, NY 10010
mackids.com

Square Fish books may be purchased for business or promotional use. For information on bulk
purchases, please contact the Macmillan Corporate and Premium Sales Department at
(800) 221-7945 x5442 or by e-mail at specialmarkets@macmillan.com.

Library of Congress Cataloging-in-Publication Data
Broach, Elise.
The miniature world of Marvin & James / Elise Broach ; illustrated by Kelly Murphy.
pages   cm. — (The masterpiece adventures ; book 1)
"Christy Ottaviano Books."
Summary: When his best friend, a human boy named James, goes away on vacation,
Marvin the beetle worries that their friendship may end.
ISBN 978-1-250-06958-0 (paperback)   ISBN 978-1-62779-204-2 (ebook)
[1. Friendship—Fiction. 2. Beetles—Fiction. 3. Human-animal relationships—Fiction.]
I. Murphy, Kelly, illustrator. II. Title. III. Title: The miniature world of Marvin and James.
PZ7.B78083Mg 2014   [Fic]—dc23   2013036081

The artist used pen and ink on Coventry Rag paper to create the illustrations for this book.

Originally published in the United States by Henry Holt and Company, LLC
First Square Fish Edition: 2015
Book designed by April Ward
Square Fish logo designed by Filomena Tuosto
1   3   5   7   9   10   8   6   4   2

AR: 2.6 / LEXILE: 330L

The Masterpiece Adventures   BOOK ONE

The Miniature World of
MARVIN & JAMES

ELISE BROACH

HYANNIS MA 02601
JUL 19
AM
2013

First-Class

USA

Illustrated by
KELLY MURPHY

SQUARE FISH

Christy Ottaviano Books
Henry Holt and Company • NEW YORK

For Jane Kamensky,
with thanks for so many years
of rich friendship
—E. B.

To adventurous Anna
—K. M.

Contents

CHAPTER ONE

James Says Good-bye

Marvin is sad.

James is going away.

"Just to the beach," James tells him.

Mrs. Pompaday and William are
going too.

Only Mr. Pompaday will stay.
Marvin does not like Mr. Pompaday.

James says, "I will be back in a week."

That does not make Marvin feel
better. A week is a long time! He will
miss James.

He rolls into a ball, like this:

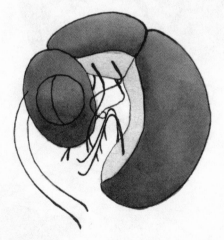

James leans close to Marvin. "Don't be sad, little guy. When I come home, I'll bring you a surprise!"

Even that does not make Marvin feel better. What will he do without James? James is his best friend.

"You can help me pack," James says.

He lifts his suitcase onto the bed.

Marvin does not want to help James

pack. But at least it is something they

can do together.

James has a list of everything he needs to pack. He puts the list on his desk.

VACATION LIST

1. Socks
2. Underwear
3. Swimsuit
4. Pajamas
5. Shirts
6. Shorts
7. Toothbrush
8. Book

"Now, when I say something, cross it off," James tells Marvin. He opens the bottle of ink on the desk. He puts the cap next to Marvin with a little ink in it.

Marvin can't read, but he is good at crossing things off. He dips his front legs in the ink.

"One," says James. "Socks." He puts socks in the suitcase.

Marvin draws a line through the first word on the list.

"Two," says James. "Underwear." He puts underwear in the suitcase.

Marvin draws a line through the second word.

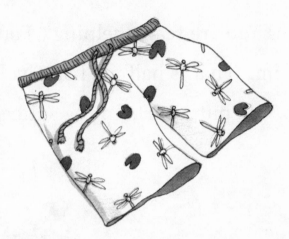

"Three . . . swimsuit." James puts his swimsuit in the suitcase. It has dragonflies on it. Marvin thinks it would look nicer with beetles. He draws a line through the third word on the list.

"Four . . . pajamas." James puts his pajamas in the suitcase.

Marvin draws a line through the fourth word.

"See? You are really helping!" James tells him. "That is half my list. Five . . . shirts." He puts shirts in the suitcase.

Oops! Marvin has no more ink on his legs. He dips them in the cap again. He draws a line through the fifth word on the list.

"Six . . . shorts. My suitcase is almost full." James squeezes his shorts into the suitcase.

Marvin draws a line through the sixth word on the list.

"Seven . . . toothbrush. I always forget my toothbrush," James tells Marvin. "That's why I made a list in the first place." He puts his toothbrush in the suitcase.

Marvin draws a line through the seventh word.

7. Toothbrush

There is only one word left.

"Eight . . . book! That's everything," says James. He takes a book from his shelf. Marvin draws a line through the last word on the list.

8. Book

"There's no room," James says. He puts the book on the floor and moves things around in the suitcase.

"James!" Mrs. Pompaday calls. "Are you ready? We can't be late for the plane."

"Coming, Mom," James says. He zips his suitcase shut.

Uh-oh! The book is still on the floor. James will forget his book! Marvin runs over the list. All the words are crossed off. He taps his legs on number eight.

James sees him. "Good job!" he says. "You crossed off everything."

Marvin keeps tapping.

James puts on his shoes.

Marvin runs around in circles.

"Don't worry," James says. "I'll be
back soon."

Marvin runs to the cap of ink and dips his legs in it.

James stands up. "Time to go."

Marvin runs back to the paper and draws this:

Finally, James understands. "Oh!" he says. "I forgot my book!"

He finds the book on the floor and puts it in his suitcase. Marvin sighs.

"Thanks, little guy!" James smiles at Marvin. "You are a big help."

He pats Marvin's shell. "Good-bye! See you in a week."

VACATION LIST
socks

Marvin lifts one leg and waves good-bye. He is still sad. But at least he helped James pack, and James did not forget his book.

CHAPTER TWO
In the Study

Marvin is bored. Without James, there is nothing to do. It has been days and days since he went away.

"Marvin, cheer up!" Mama says. James will be home soon. Why don't you draw something?"

Under the kitchen sink, where the beetles live, there is an art studio just for Marvin. James gives him paper and ink. He can draw and draw. Marvin loves making pictures. But today he just doesn't feel like it.

"I miss James," he tells Mama.

"I know, darling," Mama says. "But you have to stop moping! Only boring beetles get bored."

Marvin frowns. Mama sometimes says things that don't make sense. A boring beetle would not have an interesting life in the first place. Why would he get bored?

"I'm not boring," Marvin says in a small voice.

"I know you're not." Mama
hugs him. "So why don't you think
of something to do? Go play with
Elaine."

Elaine is Marvin's cousin. Sometimes she is fun. Sometimes she is annoying. But there is nobody else to play with, so Marvin agrees.

"Come on," Elaine says, grabbing one of Marvin's legs. "Let's have an adventure!"

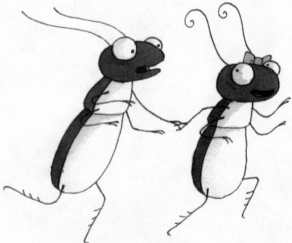

"What kind of adventure?"

"I'll show you. I found a new place for us to play."

Elaine leads the way to Mr. Pompaday's study. The beetles seldom go in there because there is no food. There is only Mr. Pompaday, working at his desk. Marvin thinks Mr. Pompaday is a good example of a boring person.

But he is not there. Today the study
is empty.

Elaine crawls up the side of the big
desk. "Marvin!" she shouts. "Look at this!"

Marvin follows her.

He sees something strange on the
desk. It's a black box with a hole in it.
Elaine climbs up the side and disappears
through the hole.

"Elaine!" Marvin cries. "Where are you?"

He can hear her laughing. "Come on!
It's fun!"

Marvin looks around. It seems safe.

He crawls up the side of the black box. It is smooth and slippery.

He peeks in the hole.

It's dark inside the box, and the air is full of dust. Marvin crawls through the hole.

He is in a short, bumpy tunnel. At the end is a big, black space. Far below, Elaine is jumping and rolling in a pile of something.

"It's so soft!" she calls to Marvin.

"What is that stuff?" Marvin asks.

"Wood!" Elaine says.

Wood? Why are there little pieces of wood in this funny black box? Marvin watches Elaine. She is doing somersaults.

"Come and see," she says. "Here, I'll show you."

She climbs back up to where Marvin is waiting.

"Look," she says. "Like this."

Elaine puts her front two legs together and dives. She flies through the air and lands with a soft *ffft!*

"Wheeeeeeee!" she shouts. "What are you waiting for?"

It does look fun.

"Okay," Marvin says. "Here I come."
He puts his front two legs together
and dives.

For a second, he is flying through
the air . . . like a butterfly or a
dragonfly or just a plain old fly. He
feels fast and free.

Then he lands in a soft pile of wood
shavings. *Ffft!* Dust rises in clouds all
around him.

"Hey, this is GREAT!" Marvin says, crawling back up the inside of the box.

"Told you so," says Elaine, following him.

"What is this thing?" Marvin asks.

"I don't know," Elaine says, "but isn't it the best?"

They perch at the edge of the tunnel, then dive, one after the other.

First Elaine does a belly flop.
Marvin copies her.

Then Marvin does a somersault.
Elaine copies him.

They jump holding hands.

They jump, then spin
three times.

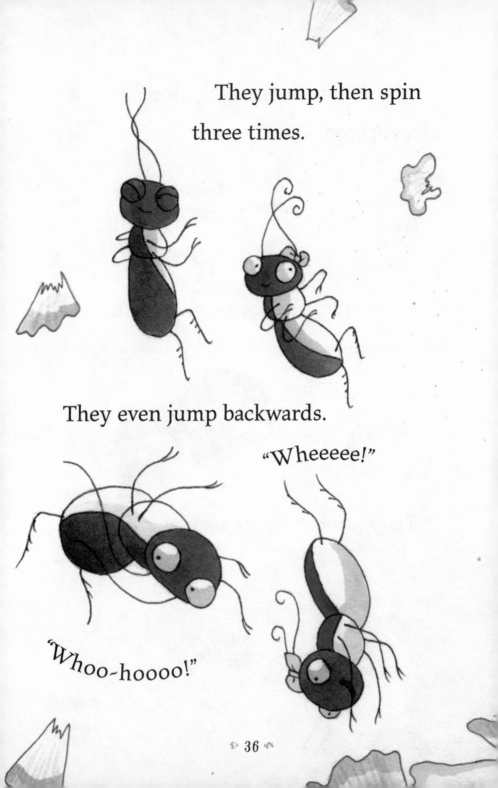

They even jump backwards.

"Wheeeee!"

"Whoo-hoooo!"

They have never had such a good
time.

As they are jumping and diving and
rolling in the soft wood shavings, they
hear a noise.

Marvin freezes. "What was that?"
he asks Elaine.

"I don't know," she says.

They hear footsteps close to the desk. A chair moves. A lamp clicks on, and light shines through the hole above them.

"It's Mr. Pompaday," Marvin whispers. "He'll hear us."

"Oh, drat!" Elaine says. "Maybe he'll go away."

They wait. They can hear Mr.
Pompaday working. He does not go
away.

"Do you think we can sneak out?"
Elaine whispers.

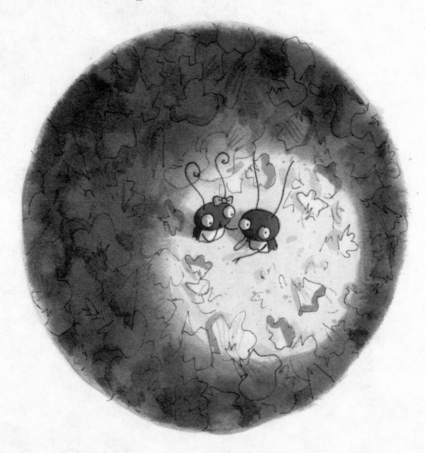

"Not if he's right there," Marvin says. "He'll see us."

"I'll climb up and find out what he's doing," Elaine says.

But as she climbs the inside wall of
the box, something comes through the
hole, completely blocking it. It is pitch-
black inside the box. And then,
suddenly, there is a very loud noise.

VWWWWRRR

The box shakes and shakes. Marvin
thinks it is going to explode.

RRRRRRRRR

CHAPTER THREE

Trapped!

Elaine is thrown off the wall, but
Marvin can't see where she lands.

There is dust everywhere. Bits of
wood fall through the air like snow.
They land on top of Marvin.

Help!

He can't see. He can't breathe. The noise goes on and on. It's the loudest noise Marvin has ever heard.

Then, just as suddenly, it stops.

Light still shines into the box, which is quiet now and cloudy with dust.

Where is Elaine?

Before Marvin can find her, something blocks the hole again. *WHIRRRRRRRRRRRRRRR!*

The shaking and the noise start up again. Marvin crawls as fast as he can to one side of the box. Here, he is safe from falling bits of wood. What in the world are they inside of?

This time when the noise stops, Marvin is ready. He runs over the pile of wood shavings. "Elaine? Elaine? Where are you?"

Three legs are poking up through the soft wood. They are waving wildly.

"It's okay. I see you," Marvin says. He grabs one of Elaine's legs and pulls her out just as the noise and shaking start again. Together, they run to the side of the box.

"What is going on?" Elaine cries.

"I don't know," Marvin says. "I'll climb up and have a look."

Marvin tries to climb the side of the box but it is shaking too much. Every time he gets an inch up the wall, he is knocked back down. The noise is so loud, his head hurts.

Then the noise and shaking stop.
The phone is ringing. Marvin hears
Mr. Pompaday say, "Hello?"

A chair scrapes the floor, and footsteps
leave the room.

Phew!

But something is still blocking the hole. There is no light in the box. Thank goodness, beetles can see in the dark.

"Let's try to get out," Marvin says.

"Okay," says Elaine. But she sounds scared.

They climb up the inside of the box.
The hole is blocked by a pointed piece
of wood. It has a dark tip.

It looks like something Marvin has
seen before. But what?

"Oh!" says Elaine. "It's a pencil."

A pencil! Suddenly, Marvin knows what the black box is. James has a little one on the desk in his bedroom. It's a machine that makes pencils sharp . . . a pencil sharpener!

"We have to get out of here," Marvin tells Elaine.

"How?" Elaine cries. "The pencil is there. Marvin—we're trapped!" She covers her face with her legs. "That hole is the only way out. Oh, Marvin! We're going to DIE!"

CHAPTER FOUR
A Way Out

"Elaine, stop that," Marvin says. He crawls along the point of the pencil. It's jammed into the hole. There's no room for a beetle to squeeze out.

"We are going to die here, all alone," Elaine sobs.

Marvin sighs. Elaine is not good in an emergency. Maybe this is the opposite of Mama's saying—exciting people always get excited.

"Elaine, you're not helping," Marvin says. "Let's try to push the pencil out."

Elaine stops crying. "Okay," she says.

She crawls up next to Marvin. They use their legs to try to move the pencil.

"Push!" Marvin says.

"I am!" Elaine says.

The pencil does not move.

"Harder," Marvin says.

"I AM!" Elaine cries.

They push with more legs.

But the pencil still does not move. It's stuck.

"Oh, Marvin, we will never get out of here! This box will become our grave." Elaine starts to cry again. "Nobody will ever find us."

"They will find us," Marvin says. "Mr. Pompaday has to pull out the pencil sometime."

"Really?" Elaine cheers up. "Do you think he will?"

"Yes," Marvin says. But he thinks to himself, *By then, it may be too late.*

They keep trying to push the pencil out of the hole, but it doesn't move. Soon they are too tired to push anymore.

"What if you're wrong?" Elaine asks.
"What if Mr. Pompaday doesn't pull
out the pencil in time?"

Here she goes, Marvin thinks.

"Our family will never see us again,"
Elaine says sadly, rolling into a ball.
"I've had a good life. Good-bye, sweet
world!"

Marvin shakes his head. "Elaine, will
you please stop?"

There has to be another way out of the box.

Marvin looks at the pencil and thinks. Far away, he can hear Mr. Pompaday talking on the phone.

"I know!" he says. "We'll EAT our way out."

Elaine looks at him. "Eat the pencil? Ewww. It's not food."

"If we chew bits off it, we can make enough room to squeeze out," Marvin tells her.

Elaine does not look happy. "Ewww," she says again.

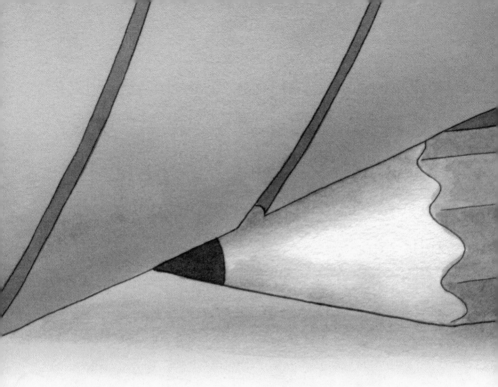

"Come on, Elaine," Marvin says. "We
have to try. You don't want to stay here
forever, do you?"

So they crawl to the place where the
pencil is stuck in the hole.

Marvin takes a small bite. The wood
is hard and dry. *Yuck!* He spits it out.

Elaine takes a bite. She makes a face
and spits it out too.

"Keep going," Marvin says.

Together, they take bites of the
pencil. *Crunch, crunch, crunch.*

"It tastes awful," Elaine says.

"I know," Marvin says. "But look!
We're making a space."

Where they have been biting the pencil, they can see a tiny sliver of light.

They keep chewing on the pencil.

"Okay, that's enough," Marvin says. He pushes the pencil to make more room. "Now try to squeeze through."

Elaine tries to crawl through the space. She can't fit.

Marvin sighs. They chew some more.

"You try," Elaine tells him. "Then you can pull me through."

So Marvin crawls over to the space. He tries to fit.

It's too tight.

He sucks in his breath and tries again.

This time, HOORAY! The pencil moves a little, and he squeezes through the hole, into the bright light of the study.

"I made it!" he cries to Elaine.

Then he hears Mr. Pompaday's

footsteps coming back.

"Hurry, Elaine!" Marvin says. He reaches into the hole and grabs her front legs. He pulls and pulls.

Elaine does not move.

He pulls harder, pressing his shell against the pencil to move it over.

Finally, POP! Elaine comes flying through the hole.

"Ow!" she says. "That hurt!"

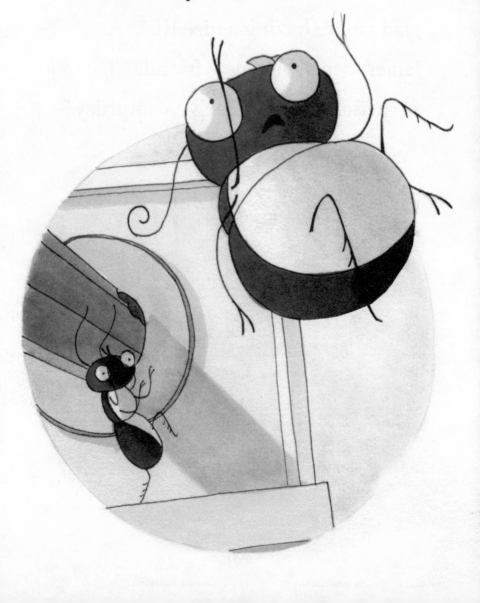

"Run," Marvin whispers. They race behind the lamp.

"Good," Mr. Pompaday is saying. "I'm glad you're having a nice time. And James made some new friends? That's a surprise. All right. See you Saturday."

Mr. Pompaday hangs up the phone and sits down.

Elaine tugs at Marvin's leg. "Come on," she whispers. "He's busy now. Let's go home."

But Marvin can't move. James has made new friends? *New* friends?

"Marvin," Elaine says, tugging his leg again. "Time to go."

Marvin follows her, but he can't stop thinking about James. He has been missing James for days now. What if James has not been missing him?

CHAPTER FIVE
Homecoming!

Safe at home, Marvin and Elaine tell the rest of the family about the black box.

"A pencil sharpener!" Papa says. "That is NO PLACE FOR BEETLES."

"No, indeed," Uncle Albert adds.

"Marvin, you are lucky you and
Elaine didn't get hurt!" Mama cries.
She hugs him close. "Promise me you
won't do that again."

"I won't, Mama," Marvin promises. But he feels a little sad. It was fun to jump and roll in the wood shavings.

The rest of the week passes by
slowly. Finally, it is Saturday. James
is coming home!

Marvin is still thinking about the
phone call. James is his best friend. But
what if James has a new best friend?
A best friend who isn't Marvin?

What if James is having so much fun, he doesn't even want to come home?

Well, there is nothing Marvin can do about that.

Mama can see that he's upset. "What is it, darling?" she asks. "Why are you sad?"

Marvin tries to tell her. "James loves the beach, Mama. He likes to swim and play in the sand. He's having a good time without me. What if he doesn't even miss me?"

"Now, Marvin," Mama says. "I'm sure James misses you. He can miss you AND have a good time at the beach."

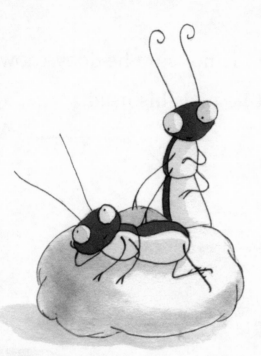

Marvin tells her about the phone
call and says gloomily, "James has new
friends now."

"But that's nice, darling," Mama says.
"James needs more friends . . . people
friends. He can have new friends and
still be friends with you. You know
that, right?"

Marvin is not sure he does know
that. But he nods his head.

Then he has an idea. He will make
a picture for James. He will make a
picture of the beach. Then James can
look at it and remember how much
fun he had.

Marvin goes to his art studio. He finds a small scrap of paper. He dips his legs in ink. He has seen the beach in books that James has, and on television. He knows just what to draw.

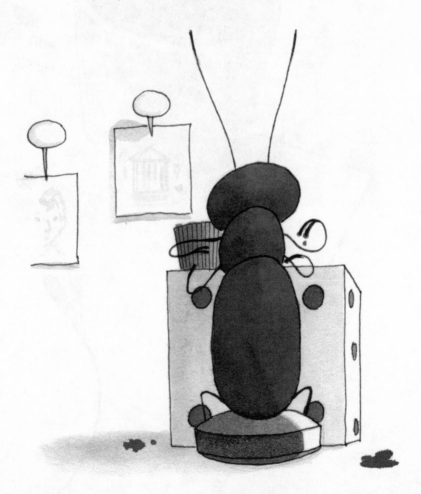

He draws waves.

He makes tiny dots for sand.

He draws a bird.

At last, he draws the sun, big in the sky, shining over everything.

It's a nice picture. Marvin hopes James will like it.

He lets it dry. Then he folds it under one leg so he can take it to James's room. He crawls all the way there and up onto the desk, where he waits for James to get home.

Around three o'clock, there is a noise in the hall. Marvin has been dozing, but now he's awake. He hears the door open. He hears William, the baby, say "Ya ya!"

James is here!

James runs into the room. He's smiling. He looks exactly the same, but his skin is a little brown. He has more freckles.

He comes right to the desk and looks for Marvin.

"There you are, little guy!" he says. He scoops Marvin onto his finger.

"What's that? A picture? Is it for me?"

James takes the paper and unfolds it.

"Wow! This is GREAT! It looks just like the beach!"

Marvin beams.

"I'll put it somewhere safe, so my mom won't find it," James says. He looks at it some more. "I wish you could have gone with me."

Marvin's heart swells. James wished he had been at the beach! Even with his new friends, he had still been thinking about Marvin.

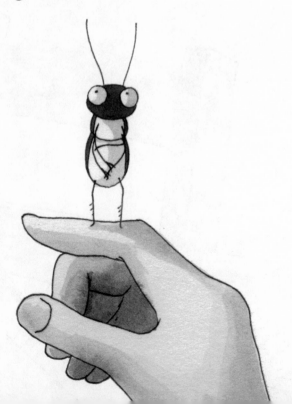

"You would have loved the beach," James says. "Oh, wait . . . I have something for you!"

James sets Marvin on the desk and reaches into his pocket.

"Here," he says. "It's your present."

It's a shell—a delicate white seashell, with stripes of pink, blue, and yellow curling all around it. James puts it on the desk.

Marvin crawls over to look at it. It is beautiful.

"You can go inside," James tells him. "It can be like a secret hideout for you."

Marvin crawls into the shell. Inside is a smooth, curving tunnel. Marvin goes deeper and deeper.

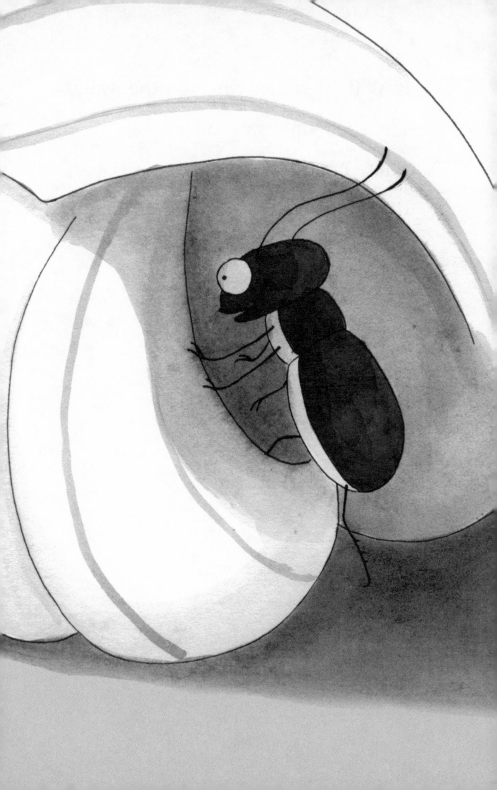

Pink light comes through the walls.

The shell smells of salt.

There is no sound.

It is like being in another world.

"Do you like it?" James asks, his voice far away.

Marvin loves it. He thinks about how James found this shell on the beach and carried it all the way home, just for him.

Marvin crawls out of the shell.

James smiles at him. "I missed you," he says.

And even though Marvin is so happy that James is home, it is a good feeling to be missed. It's like the feeling of being someone's best friend . . . because it means nobody can take your place. There is nobody else in the whole world as special as you are.

And then Marvin smiles. Because now he knows something. You can only be missed when someone goes away!

When Marvin the beetle goes collecting with his family, Uncle Albert gets hurt. Marvin needs James's help to save Uncle Albert. Can he find him in time?

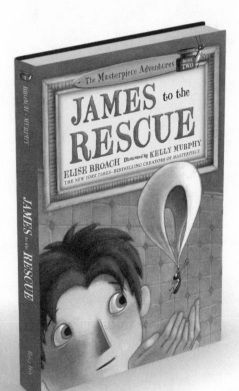

Keep reading for a sneak peek.

CHAPTER ONE

Collecting

Marvin is excited. Papa and Uncle Albert are going collecting. Collecting is what the beetles call it when they crawl around the Pompadays' apartment looking for things they can use.

A button can make a pretty table.

A doll's shoe can be a nice chair.

A cap from a tube of toothpaste can hold a giant feast.

For the first time ever, Marvin and Elaine get to go collecting. There's no telling what they will find. They are so excited that they do a happy dance, like this:

Mama is not so excited.

"Please be careful," she says. "Collecting is dangerous! You must listen to Papa and Uncle Albert."

"We will," Marvin promises.

"We're going to have the BEST time!" Elaine says. "I know we'll find something really good."

"I hope so," Marvin says.

Marvin thinks about what he would like to find.

He might find part of a crayon . . .

Or a tiny piece of wrapping paper . . .

Or something to put inside his secret
hideout.

"Ready?" Papa says.

"YES!" Marvin and Elaine shout.

Papa and Uncle Albert have a little
sack that they drag by the string. It's
blue and silky. It used to hold a pair of
Mrs. Pompaday's earrings. Now it's the
perfect bag for collecting.

"Let's go," says Uncle Albert.

Papa, Uncle Albert, Marvin, and Elaine sneak out of their home in the kitchen cupboard.

William, James's baby brother, is in the kitchen. He's banging a spoon on the floor.

Bang! Bang! Bang!

The beetles do not like William. They hide near the leg of a chair.

But William sees them.

"Ba ba!" William says.

Uh-oh! He crawls across the floor, banging his spoon.

BANG! BANG! BANG!

The beetles race away from him.

William crawls after them.

"BA BA!" he yells.

William raises his spoon over their heads.

"Stop, drop, and roll!" Papa cries.

The beetles all roll into little balls.

e sees something else,

at Elaine is already racing

l speed.

shiny.

silver.

But then they hear Mrs. Pompaday.

"Shhhh, William," she says. "It's time for your nap."

William starts to cry. She picks him up and carries him away, her high heels clicking on the floor.

Click, click, click.

"Phew!" says Uncle Albert. "That was a close one. Let's go to James's room."

"Wait," Elaine says. "I found something."

Marv
but tho
beetles

But then h
something th
toward at ful
Something
Something